Come back,
Grandma

For Betsy and Man S.L.
For Lily Fernanda C.M.

A Red Fox Book

Published by Random House Children's Books
20 Vauxhall Bridge Road, London SW1V 2SA

A division of Random House UK Ltd
London Melbourne Sydney Auckland
Johannesburg and agencies throughout the world

1 3 5 7 9 10 8 6 4 2

First published in Great Britain in 1993 by
The Bodley Head Children's Books

Red Fox edition 1995

Printed in China

RANDOM HOUSE UK Limited Reg. No. 954009

ISBN 0 09 921951 4

Come back, Grandma

Sue Limb

Pictures by Claudio Muñoz

Red Fox

Bessie loved her daddy

but he was a radio fanatic.

Bessie loved her mummy

but she was too busy to play.

Bessie's brother Olly was too small
and smelly to be much fun.

And Krishna next door wasn't allowed out much.

But Bessie had Grandma.

Grandma had speckled eyes like birds' eggs, bendy thumbs
and a crinkle at the top of her nose.

Grandma could do tricks with cards.

She could tame birds.

Grandma and Bessie played hide and seek.

They played hopscotch.

But Bessie's favourite game was Count Grandma's Freckles.

Grandma always had time for Bessie.

But one day Grandma got ill and died.

Bessie missed Grandma.

She missed her bendy thumbs and her speckled eyes and
the crinkle at the top of her nose.

Sometimes at night Bessie thought she could see
Grandma's face in the pattern of the curtain. But in the
morning it was gone.

Bessie's mother said Grandma had gone to heaven. 'Where's heaven?' asked Bessie. 'Can she ring us up?'

Bessie looked at the stars at night, trying to see heaven, but all she saw were the lights of aeroplanes.

Daddy said Grandma was now part of Nature: the trees and the flowers. Bessie saw Grandma's face in a tree once, but when she looked again it was gone.

Krishna next door said Grandma might be born again as an animal or a bird. Bessie looked hard at all the animals she saw, but they didn't look much like Grandma, although she did see a baby chimpanzee once who looked just like Olly.

Bessie grew up, but she still missed her grandma sometimes.

Bessie got married and had a baby.
The baby was a girl. They called her Rose and they loved her.

At first Rose looked just like any other baby, but as she grew
up into a little girl, Bessie noticed something. Rose had
green speckled eyes like birds' eggs. She had bendy thumbs
and a crinkle at the top of her nose. When she was three
she got her first freckles.

When she was five she started to tame birds. She was just like
Grandma, only a little girl. She stopped Bessie feeling sad.

Because, suddenly, it was as if Grandma
had never been away.

Some bestselling Red Fox picture books

THE BIG ALFIE AND ANNIE ROSE STORYBOOK
by Shirley Hughes
OLD BEAR
by Jane Hissey
OI! GET OFF OUR TRAIN
by John Burningham
DON'T DO THAT!
by Tony Ross
NOT NOW, BERNARD
by David McKee
ALL JOIN IN
by Quentin Blake
THE WHALES' SONG
by Gary Blythe and Dyan Sheldon
JESUS' CHRISTMAS PARTY
by Nicholas Allan
THE PATCHWORK CAT
by Nicola Bayley and William Mayne
MATILDA
by Hilaire Belloc and Posy Simmonds
WILLY AND HUGH
by Anthony Browne
THE WINTER HEDGEHOG
by Ann and Reg Cartwright
A DARK, DARK TALE
by Ruth Brown
HARRY, THE DIRTY DOG
by Gene Zion and Margaret Bloy Graham
DR XARGLE'S BOOK OF EARTHLETS
by Jeanne Willis and Tony Ross
WHERE'S THE BABY?
by Pat Hutchins